THE BOOK OF SPINJITZU

"YOU ARE ONLY AT THE BEGINNING,
AND THE ROAD IS LONG AND WINDING."

I have studied Spinjitzu all my life, but there will always
be more to learn. My Father, the First Spinjitzu
Master, taught me the ways of Spinjitzu and the wonders
of Ninjago — the world he created. Since I was a boy I have
recorded these lessons so that I may teach others. Parts of
this book are from journals I kept as a child and as a young
man (yes, I was young once!) and others have been added as
I have continued my studies. I have also commented on the pages
whilst reading this book again later on in life ...

To be in possession of *The Book of Spinjitzu* is to have great
responsibility. The information it contains is to be used wisely,
and only for good. It is my hope that the reader will let the
power of Spinjitzu unlock the true potential within them to become
one of Ninjago Island's great champions. And, should I not be here
tomorrow, this is my legacy ...

— Master Wu

THE PHILOSOPHY OF SPINJITZU

"NOT ALL LESSONS ARE ABOUT FIGHTING."

The first thing my Father told my older brother Garmadon and me, was that Spinjitzu is more than an ancient martial art of punches, kicks, flips and throws - it is a philosophy of living that takes a lifetime's journey to acquire. My greatest desire at the time was that Father would teach us how to defeat the forces of evil. Though I would indeed learn how to do this, I would go on to learn so much more.

BALANCE

Spinjitzu is about balance. Not just how a ninja stands as he fights, but also how he balances the light and darkness (good and bad) within himself and the world around him.

Spinjitzu is also the art of Rotation, which is core to how a ninja moves. It broadens perspective and teaches flexibility during battle and in life, which is full of change. Rotation adds force and momentum to blows and is a source of strength. Once mastered, it helps a ninja create an elemental tornado and it also comes in handy whilst dancing!

ROTATION

Spinjitzu mirrors the qualities of who is studying it. Only a true Spinjitzu Master knows that human potential goes far beyond what most people can imagine. Spinjitzu is a quest for total perfection. It may not be reached, but the value is in the trying.

I was very young when my Father explained that Garmadon and I needed to uphold and pass on the legacy of Spinjitzu. For a boy, being asked to take on such responsibility was daunting. From the beginning, I took my studies very seriously. I did not want to let my Father down.

MASTER CLASS

*"TO BECOME A TRUE NINJA, FIRST YOU MUST BE ABLE
TO SEE WHAT OTHERS DO NOT SEE."*

One day, I will be a ninja! Our Father says being a ninja is one of the best things you can be. A ninja is honourable and strong. A ninja never quits and never leaves a friend behind. A ninja helps those who need it, and keeps dark forces from spreading evil. Look out, dark forces, soon I will be coming for you! (As long as they're not too dark, I still leave the light on when I go to sleep.)

Garmadon and I enjoy watching Father and hearing him tell stories about Ninjago Island long before time had a name. I want to grow up to be just like him. He is so graceful and calm, except when Garmadon and I fight. Brothers should not fight, Father says.

Even if I am never to be the master that he is, I know I will learn many things. As Father likes to say, "The journey is more important than the destination." I am excited to see how far I can go on my journey.

MASTER OF SPINJITZU!

I can't wait to begin my training!

Little did I know what I was in for next!

GARMADON

WU (ME)

TRAINING DAYS

Training is hard! I didn't think it would be like this. When the training sessions are over I am so tired I can barely lift my chopsticks to eat!

Before sunrise, Garmadon and I stretch our arms, legs, necks, shoulders, backs and even our eyes and ears. Father says stretching loosens the body and mind for the challenges ahead.

NECK STRETCHES   LEG STRETCHES

????

Then, we run the training course Father has built. Something always smashes, throws us or trips us! Father just drinks his tea, and says, "Fail," every time we fall. Then, we do it again.

Next, Father leads us through Spinjitzu movements. However many we learn, it seems there are a thousand more. Sometimes I want to give up, but then I remember, "A ninja never quits." (Although sometimes a ninja BADLY wants to!)

It was the Great Devourer that took my brother away from me.

Yesterday, something scary happened. During our training exercises my katana was knocked over the monastery wall. Garmadon went to bring it back, but when he reached for it he was bitten by a strange snake. Father and I were very worried, for a great evil had found its way into my brother's heart. The snake's venom could turn the purest of things wicked ...

FINDING YOUR TRUE POTENTIAL

"SPINJITZU IS INSIDE EACH AND EVERY ONE OF US. BUT IT WILL ONLY BE UNLOCKED WHEN THE KEY IS READY TO BE FOUND."

Over the last few years, Garmadon and I have taken many steps in our study of Spinjitzu. Father says that to reach a higher level of mastery, we must unlock our True Potential. In each of us, there are obstacles and worries that keep us from true greatness. Only when we conquer those obstacles, will our hearts be free and our personal True Potential (an elemental power or a skill) be unlocked. Once True Potential is reached, we will reach a state of mind that will let us achieve higher goals and higher levels of Spinjitzu mastery.

DOUBT   FAILING   EMBARRASSMENT

Me (trying to be brave)

Fear is what most often prevents an aspiring ninja from making that step forward. I wonder what my greatest fear is? Doubt? Failing?

Father says that True Potential unlocks the power of Elemental Masters. What must I do to unlock my True Potential? What is my True Potential? When I have reached it, which element will I be connected to? Fire, Ice, Lightning, Earth? Am I an Elemental Master at all? How will I be able to help Father protect our world from evil? I hope the future holds the answers ...

CURRENT ELEMENTAL MASTERS:

Pale Man — Light
Griffin Turner — Speed
Skylor — Amber
Bolobo — Nature
Karlof — Metal
Gravis — Gravity

Neuro — Mind
Ash — Smoke
Jacob — Sound
Chamille — Form
Tox — Poison

Kai — Fire
Cole — Earth
Zane — Ice
Jay — Lightning
Nya — Water

Agent of Evil

Me, Elemental Master of ????

THE JOURNEY TO MASTERY

"ONLY A TRUE SPINJITZU MASTER KNOWS THAT THE HUMAN POTENTIAL EXCEEDS WHAT WE DARE TO IMAGINE."

Every morning, I ask Father, "Have we reached our True Potential yet?" But he always answers, "When you do, you will be the first to know about it!" But how? There is so much I still do not understand. I must work hard and study even harder.

Garmadon is becoming less interested in unlocking his True Potential on his journey to mastering Spinjitzu. He does not follow instructions and will not practise by himself. He has changed. A darkness is pushing him away from the path our Father hoped he would take.

I train each day to harness not just my physical potential with Spinjitzu movements, but also my mental potential by studying their meaning. Everything in Spinjitzu is done for a reason and every movement and thought has a purpose. The combinations of these are too many to count, but by understanding them all I will continue my lifelong path towards mastering Spinjitzu.

"Life is but a series of small steps towards your ultimate goal," Father likes to say. But I must admit, on many days, it feels like we are walking backwards!

SPINJITZU IN EVERYDAY LIFE

"SPINJITZU IS AS MUCH A PART OF EVERYTHING YOU DO AS BREATHING."

Father says many Spinjitzu movements involve rotation, or turning. The Spinjitzu Tornado is one of these movements. Father challenged us to find examples of rotations in everyday life. Here are some:

We stir tea in the teapot to make the sugar dissolve.

Do not use excessive force when stirring, or the tea spills!

We turn around to speak to someone behind us.

Pottery wheels rotate so we can make pots and vases.

It's best to talk to one person at a time!

Executed properly, rotation can help us create true pieces of art.

How will this training help me to create my first Spinjitzu Tornado? I must meditate on that and practise harder, because when I use Spinjitzu in battle, my moves should be quick and precise. I'm sure that practising the art of stirring tea will be an excellent start.

MY FIRST SPINJITZU TORNADO

Today, Garmadon and I created our first Spinjitzu Tornadoes! It was AMAZING!

Father sent us to the village to fetch tea. While we were there, bullies confronted us and tried to take the tea. Without thinking, we put our training to use. The next thing we knew, we were in the centre of whirlwinds that seemed to blow our enemies half way to the Lost City of Ouroborus!

The Spinjitzu Tornado is one of the most important moves to master, and being able to perform one is a huge sign that we are learning a lot!

Created with precise motions, the Spinjitzu Tornado is a shield of energy embracing the ninja, creating a devastating vessel for an attack. The following moves led me to a Spinjitzu Tornado:

1. I shout "NINJA-GO!" – this helps me concentrate and attain inner balance.

2. I initiate a series of precise movements that build up momentum. This increases as I advance to rotational movements. It is like one balanced motion. Almost a dance.

3. Having achieved perfect balance, I then have an unstoppable whirl of energy surrounding me.

4. I maintain the pace, without losing force, and each of my blows will be equally strong. At first I feel a bit dizzy ...

5. I've created a Spinjitzu Tornado! I slow down, concentrate and do it all over again. Practice makes perfect!

THE PROPHECY OF THE GREEN NINJA

"ONE NINJA WILL RISE ABOVE THE OTHERS ..."

What's _my_ destiny? Is my life's mission to become the Green Ninja? Or maybe it will be to _find_ the Green Ninja and protect _him?_

"One ninja will Rise above the others and become the Green Ninja – the ninja destined to defeat the Dark Lord." So says the Prophecy of the Green Ninja. I have not been able to stop thinking about it since I first heard it from my Father.

The Green Ninja is the most powerful of all the ninja. It is said he will be Revealed only when the Four Golden Weapons of Spinjitzu are laid out before him. It is also said that the weapons will Recognize him. I wonder what that means? Will they say, "Hello, Green Ninja?" Somehow, I do not think so.

16

The Dark Lord is the Overlord, the eternal, indestructible enemy of all things good, a being born of pure darkness who was created when the first shadow fell, after my Father formed the world of Ninjago with the Golden Weapons.

Once the Green Ninja is found, he must be protected, as one day he will save us all. The Overlord's Dark Forces will want to keep the Green Ninja from mastering his powers and they will stop at nothing to accomplish their goal.

Actually, the Golden Weapons react to the presence of the Green Ninja by glowing green.

THE DARK SIDE OF SPINJITZU

"SPINJITZU IS A SWORD WITH TWO BLADES."

Father says Spinjitzu, if not done exactly right, can cause great harm. I learned that lesson today. During sparring, I rotated my hips too much and too quickly while executing a Kick of the Mantis, and I accidentally sent Garmadon flying through a support post. The entire roof almost came down on him!

Garmadon lashed out at me afterwards with a kind of anger I had never seen from him. In his fury, he was not using Spinjitzu correctly and nearly destroyed the entire monastery before Father was able to calm him. These days, it seems there is almost as much darkness in Garmadon as light and nothing our Father has tried will reverse it.

Father understood that my brother needed different training, which would help him return to the right track. He told me that using Spinjitzu for evil purposes could affect the balance between good and evil and that whoever gave in to that temptation could destroy the world.

I will not let that happen to me.

THE SCROLL OF FORBIDDEN SPINJITZU

"SOME SECRETS ARE BEST LEFT HIDDEN IN THE SHADOWS."

Once, we were browsing Father's library, hoping to find a cookbook to replace Father's usual "plain noodles." Pulling out a book called *The Art of Broth*, Garmadon noticed a scroll of black paper fall. He picked it up and said it felt hot. He wanted to read it. I sensed we should not. Garmadon started to unroll the scroll when Father raced in and snatched it. He told us never to touch "the Scroll of Forbidden Spinjitzu."
Then he ordered us to leave.

The next day, Garmadon returned to the library. He said the scroll was 'calling' him. I should have told Father, instead I followed Garmadon. But the scroll wasn't there, much to Garmadon's frustration ... and my relief.

Sometimes I wake at night and see Garmadon is out of bed. I imagine he is looking for the scroll. I cannot imagine what dark secrets lie in it. A long-forgotten phrase that will turn the sun cold? A chant that will raise the spirits of the departed? A great broth recipe?

Days later, Garmadon found the scroll. We were simply blown away by what it contained! Here's what the dark secrets revealed:

It was wrong of me to steal from my Father. Much later, I realised I should not have revealed any of it in this book. So I took it out. This knowledge should be kept secret forever, but I was too young to understand then ...

TWO BROTHERS, TWO PATHS

"LEARN, PRACTISE, APPLY – IT'S THE ONLY WAY TO DISCOVER YOUR PATH."

As part of our training, Father has sent Garmadon and me out to explore the world we live in, so that we might experience the wonders of the world he created, meet its people, and learn of some of the challenges we will face as defenders of the world of Ninjago. "You cannot protect what you do not understand," he says.

I hope that our trip will renew the closeness that I felt to Garmadon when we were younger. I can see in his eyes that he is fighting the growing evil coursing through his veins. Perhaps our journey will slow, or even stop, the progress of that evil. I hope so.

I don't know where destiny will lead us, but we have made a list of adventures that should be waiting for us out there (or at least we hope they are).

1. A trip to see the statues of the heroes in Ninjago Island's history at the Corridor of Elders. (Important: must pack mountaineering gear.)

2. A climb to the top of the Wailing Alps to admire the views (earplugs needed).

3. Cross-terrain racing with Treehorns in the Birchwood Forest (Garmadon swears they exist!)

4. A seafood dinner in the City of Stiix (I love regional cuisine).

5. A trip to the Holy City of Domu (Father has recommended quite a few good reads from the city's famous library).

We were so young and naive, but also brave and eager. Though we set out on the same journey, our paths would soon take us far from each other in every way.

THE GOLDEN WEAPONS OF SPINJITZU

"THE GOLDEN WEAPONS ARE THE FOUR PILLARS ON WHICH THE WORLD OF NINJAGO STANDS."

It has been many years since I've written in my journal. Keeping the promise I gave to my Father, whom I miss dearly, I'm continuing my work.

Father has gone to his eternal rest, leaving Garmadon and me to safeguard the Golden Weapons of Spinjitzu. It was not long before my brother gave in to the evil urges inside him. He tried to take the weapons to use them and Spinjitzu to bend the world of Ninjago to his will. I could not allow it.

My brother, Lord Garmadon

We fought, brother against brother. I used everything I had learned about Spinjitzu and all the energy I had to stop Garmadon. I prevailed. When it was over ... I had banished my brother into the darkness of the Underworld from where no one has ever returned.

The Golden Weapons are the most powerful weapons of creation known to man. The safety of our world is entirely in my hands, so I must put aside grieving over the loss of my brother, and do my best to protect the weapons.

Each weapon lets the user channel the power of its element.

Wielded by a skilled Master of Spinjitzu, these weapons can also create amazing machines. Many years later, my ninja team found this power extremely useful in battles with the evil Serpentine tribes.

The Scythe of Quakes grants power over the earth. It can cut the hardest stone, bring about earthquakes and create deep cracks in the ground.

The Sword of Fire allows the user control over flames and heat. True to its name, it can become a blade of flame and project fire-bolts.

The Shurikens of Ice are bladed throwing stars that freeze what they touch, and project beams of ice. Afterwards, they return to the guardian of the weapon.

The Nunchucks of Lightning — a short chain connecting two dragon-headed batons that can be swung rapidly to create energy storms and project lightning bolts.

THE TRUST FACTOR

"A NINJA TRUSTS FEW, BUT TRUSTS THEM COMPLETELY."

My duties as protector of the Realm of Ninjago are such that I cannot spend every moment with the Golden Weapons of Spinjitzu. And yet, it is only a matter of time before the forces of darkness will try to get their greedy hands on them. I know and I fear that this will come sooner than I expect.

Skulkins in the service of my evil brother ...

Therefore, I have hidden the weapons separately and posted special guardians to protect them. Should anything happen to me, I have created a map to the weapons and given it to a trusted friend, Ray, and his wife, Maya.

Father said to know someone well before trusting them. A ninja decides whether to trust someone, not on the basis of their words, which can be false, but on their actions. Actions, Father felt, reveal if a person is good or not. Ray and Maya's actions have never shown them to be anything other than good, honourable people who care for others and for the world of Ninjago.

(I also like their children very much. Kai and Nya are capable of great things. I look forward to our paths crossing again in the future.)

Future heroes!

After our paths crossed once more ...

THE NINJA OF TOMORROW

"THE PAST IS THE PAST, BUT THERE IS ALWAYS THE FUTURE."

In the years between journal entries, I tried a little teaching, grew very impressive facial hair and studied.

While meditating yesterday, Eventuali-tea showed me a vision of the future that revealed my brother, Lord Garmadon, returning from the Underworld! The world of Ninjago is in terrible peril and I am afraid I might not be able to protect it on my own.

READING LIST FOR STUDY

1. Bamboo Staff Attacks and Defences
2. Spinjitzu Tornado Techniques
3. Ancient Tea Recipes
4. Guide to the Serpentine Tribes
5. Moustache Maintenance
6. The Art of the Silent Fist
7. Legends of the Temple of Fortitude

But upholding Father's legacy is paramount. The time has come to seek help, to find four chosen ones to become ninja who will wield the Golden Weapons of Spinjitzu in the fight against my brother. The new heroes could be anywhere, but I have some ideas of where to begin my quest. I must leave the monastery and begin my search immediately ...

THE CHOSEN ONES

After weeks of searching, I have found the four young people I believe are destined to be the ninja who will protect the Four Golden Weapons of Spinjitzu. Each has a great potential waiting to be unlocked. It is my responsibility to help them become what they are meant to be.

Cole tested himself by climbing one of the tallest mountains on Ninjago Island, and I met him at the peak. (I am a very fast climber!) Something was troubling Cole and he was fighting it on the inside. Cole always wants to be the best at everything. When I told him of the potential I saw in him, he was eager to study to become a ninja and Master of Spinjitzu.

Jay Walker was testing mechanical wings of his own design when he crashed in front of me. He is energetic, funny and tends to hide his insecurities behind jokes. But he doesn't hide his desire to help others. Jay will become the Lightning Ninja.

I found Zane at the bottom of a frozen pond, trying to see how long he could hold his breath. (The fish around him were eager to learn the answer as well!) Quiet, cool and logical, the aspiring Ice Ninja knows little of his past, but I see a bright future for him.

Zane could hold his breath longer than anyone suspected ... But we wouldn't learn why for a long while yet!

Kai joined the team as the future Fire Ninja. I met Kai again when he and his sister Nya fought off Skulkin Raiders sent by Lord Garmadon to retrieve the map to the Golden Weapons that was hidden in their father's forge.

After being kidnapped and escaping, Nya joined her brother to train at the monastery.

Now I must train these very different personalities in the art of Spinjitzu, help them master the abilities they will unlock, and mould them into a team ... They can only protect the world of Ninjago from the dire threats to come if they work together.

TEAM SPIRIT

"THE BEST WAY TO DEFEAT AN ENEMY IS TO MAKE HIM YOUR FRIEND."

Cole, Jay, Zane and Kai have begun their training together. They need to learn how to wield their weapons and become skilled at Spinjitzu techniques. It is taking some time for Kai to fit in. He and Cole are especially competitive and rarely see eye to eye.

Sipping tea and saying 'Fail' as they struggle through training, like my Father did to me, makes me smile on the inside.

They must not see each other as rivals or enemies. Every team member must trust that the team is there for them, no matter the situation. Trust only comes with knowing the true heart of another over time.

Jay originally wanted his weapon to look like the one he used in his favourite video game!

My ninja understand the great responsibility that rests on their shoulders. Protecting the Ninjago Realm from evil requires skills, determination and power. What they still need to discover is that each of them is an Elemental Master. If all goes well, soon they will unlock their True Potential.

They remind me of me when I was younger ... excited, eager and in need of discipline!

SPINJITZU TRAINING PROGRAMME

"EVEN LESSONS LEARNED THE HARD WAY ARE LESSONS LEARNED."

I have taught many ninja over the years. At first, it was not easy and I made mistakes. But over time, I found the combination of exercises and moves that created the best Spinjitzu training programme. Some of those are described here.

LEG WARM-UP

1. Taking a wide stance, lunge to the left, then to the right.
2. Lift one leg straight up in front of you without bending your back. Repeat with other leg.
3. Holding onto something, lift one leg behind you as high as you can. Repeat with other leg.
4. Lift and swing one leg forwards and backwards. Repeat with other leg.

<u>Balance is key in every Spinjitzu movement.</u>
<u>Finding balance is everything!</u>

IMPORTANT: Never try any of these moves without a trained Spinjitzu Master.

ARM WARM-UP

Swing arms forward, then backwards, and finally swing one arm forward and the other backwards.

Each exercise was repeated ten times.

HEAD WARM-UP

1. Turn head slowly to the left as far as you can, then to the right.
2. Slowly bring head down towards chest, then tip it back as far as you can.

HIP WARM-UP

1. Stand, feet firmly on the ground, arms stretched out at shoulder height.
2. Twist body from side to side, as if it is a wet cloth being wrung out.
3. Repeat the movement with hands on hips.

At first, my students said the exercises were "a waste of time." But after a week's training, they changed their minds and were a lot more flexible!

A strong defence is the best attack. Spinjitzu teaches us to be peaceful. These stances — if properly performed — may, in many cases, be enough to make the opponent withdraw.

PINCHED CRAB

1. Standing with feet apart, facing forwards.

2. Legs are bent at knees.

3. Arms are raised to shoulder height.

4. Hands are held like crab pincers.

BALANCE!!!

Father's original version called for feet to face forward. After seeing many students trip, I suggested feet face to the side for better balance.

An excellent move for distracting opponents.

SWOOPING CRANE

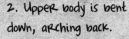

1. Arms are held out to sides, palms down.

2. Upper body is bent down, arching back.

3. Head needs to be brought up slowly.

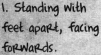

TIGER CLAW

Father's original version had closed hands, and he called it, "Hammerhead Strike." To me, it seemed more catlike, so I made the claw change.

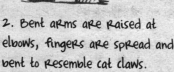

1. Standing with legs bent, feet shoulder-width apart.

2. Bent arms are raised at elbows, fingers are spread and bent to resemble cat claws.

3. Upper body is lunged forwards and down, hands held out in front.

CURIOUS DRAGON

Roar loudly to intimidate your opponent.

1. Standing with feet together, facing forwards.

2. Arms raised above head, hands are brought together, fingers facing forwards.

3. Neck needs to be thrust forward and head must lean to one side, as though puzzled.

STINGING WASP

Good attack position, but also good for dodging as you can leap to either side or back.

1. Legs are bent at knees, keeping feet together.

2. Upper body leans forward, over knees.

3. Arms are extended in front, palms together.

The key to mastering the following sequences is keeping <u>balance</u> whilst performing each rotational movement.

IMPORTANT: Do not attempt to perform these movements without the supervision of an experienced Spinjitzu Master!

SIDE ROUNDHOUSE SWING

1. Ninja stands with knees bent, one foot in front of the other.

2. Ninja turns at waist.

3. Ninja quickly turns back, bringing back foot up and around. Then they drive rear knee towards target.

Nya amazed the other ninja with her skill in this sequence!

SEE-SAW

1. TEAMWORK: Two teammates stand back-to-back and interlock elbows.

2. Ninja A bends forwards. Ninja B, on ninja A's back, kicks their legs straight out to strike.

3. Ninja B bends forwards. Ninja A, on ninja B's back, kicks their legs straight out in opposite direction.

Kai and Jay were particularly keen on practising this move.

GRASSHOPPER JUMP

1. Ninja bends knees and crouches as low to the ground as possible.

2. From crouch, ninja extends arms above head, with hands in fists.

3. Ninja springs straight up.

My students were in a hurry to learn "more complicated" moves. Long after, they were surprised how often they still use these basic blocks and attacks!

TORNADO FIST ATTACK

1. Ninja forward-punches the air, constantly rotating their shoulder joint. Ninja holds back the other arm to harvest more energy.

2. The opposite arm repeats the move.

3. Ninja delivers every punch with full force and speed, creating a 'wall' of fists.

This powerful technique is strictly to be used for defence only, to get the upper hand in battle when conflict is unavoidable.

1. DO NOT begin a training session without having stretched first!

I always keep bandages and ice packs near training areas in case of injury!

2. DO NOT begin a training session with a teammate unless you are sure the teammate is ready!

SUGGESTION: Begin all training sessions with a teammate by yelling, "Training begins now!"

3. DO NOT end a training session with a teammate until you both agree the session is over!

SUGGESTION: End all training sessions with a teammate by yelling, "Training is over."

Show respect for your opponent. You need them to train with you another day.

4. DO NOT be overconfident!

Always wear safety gear when practising, with or without weapons!

5. DO NOT attempt a new move or use a new weapon until your teacher says you are ready!

Enjoy yourself! Remember that exercising should be fun, so avoid overtraining.

6. DO NOT leave behind a teammate having difficulty with an obstacle!

Four arms and four legs can overcome an obstacle twice as easily as two arms and two legs.

NINJA AND THE GOLDEN WEAPONS

"A RAZOR-SHARP WEAPON IS AN EXTENSION OF A RAZOR-SHARP MIND."

Since my students found the map I entrusted to Ray and used it to reclaim the Golden Weapons, I feel that I have been reunited with a piece of my past. It is good to see the weapons in use once more, for the betterment of all Ninjago Island.

The ninja have been practising with the Golden Weapons, with varying degrees of success thus far.

Cole has learned how to slam the blade of the Scythe of Quakes into the ground to create tremors. However, he must come to understand that, when not in use, the Scythe should be set on the floor very gently. Otherwise, his teammates could be in for a big surprise, as Jay found out one night.

Zane has nearly perfected the use of the Shurikens of Ice. His aim still needs a little work, however. Three of my best teapots have been ruined since his practising began.

Jay's progress with the Nunchucks of Lightning has been rapid. He has gone from tangling himself in the chain in his earliest attempts, to being skilled at using the weapon for both attack and defence. Jay has also learned how to use the Nunchucks to provide power to his video game system during a blackout.

Kai took to the Sword of Fire as though he was born to wield it. (Actually, he was.) He has incinerated many of my training mannequins and developed a "wall of flame" defence shield to discourage would-be attackers.

NINJA TRANSPORT

"A NINJA IS ALWAYS WHERE HE NEEDS TO BE."

While meditating last night, I had a vision of advanced ninja machinery. I usually tell my students that their most powerful weapons in Spinjitzu are their bodies and minds, while robots and intricate machines are for the samurai. However, the future ninja will need fast vehicles because they'll have to face challenges in the farthest reaches of Ninjago Island.

Destiny's Bounty

It's a good thing none of the ninja are prone to seasickness. Or airsickness!

The first vehicle I envisioned, the Destiny's Bounty, actually exists. This flying ship was the base for the feared pirate, Captain Soto. When Soto was defeated years ago, the ruined Destiny's Bounty came to rest in the Sea of Sand. I wonder what it would take to renovate the ship so my students might use it if the occasion arose?

I imagine Jay Riding a fast motorcycle capable of travelling over any terrain, with speed boosted by Jay's elemental power of lightning.

Desert Lightning

Samurai Mech

In my vision, I don't know what the desert has to do with the vehicle. Will Jay find it there? Will it be built there? Time will tell ...

I dreamed about a massive robotic suit that can fly. It had missiles, a giant katana, and a net for capturing enemies. The robot resembled a samurai, but I could not see who was piloting it. Very frustrating!

45

Ultra Stealth Raider

This vehicle would be perfect for adventures where the ninja need to remain undetected, such as a rescue mission. According to my vision, however, it may come into my students' possession through unexpected circumstances.

First I saw a blurred image of a vehicle abandoned in a dreadful place, with dark energy running through its mechanical veins. Then a ninja appeared in the cockpit and his elemental power drove the darkness out of the machine. Now I see the Tumbler in great detail, but one very puzzling question remains ... Who is the Titanium Ninja?

Titanium Ninja Tumbler

Looking back now, I feel foolish for not immediately working it out!

Jay Walker One

This vehicle came to me in
a few lightning-fast flashes. I saw
a scientist working in a modern lab, pieces
of machinery being put together, a blue roadster speeding through the streets of Ninjago City
and some greenish semi-transparent creatures (ghosts?) being chased and swallowed by the
vehicle. I'm sure I saw Jay behind the wheel.

I envisioned this robust jet being secretly
constructed in the dark corridors of a
mystery place I was not able to identify.
Although I have never been fond of vehicles,
I felt this one would help its pilot escape
from grave danger.

Boulder Blaster

Much later it turned out I was right. Cole
used the jet to break out of Master Chen's
underground noodle factory!

DRAGONS: LEGENDARY AND REAL

"A LEGEND CAN BE A TRUTH NO ONE HAS SEEN."

My students' dragons flew away today and have not returned. Perhaps they have flown to the Spirit Coves to shed their skin? If so, what will they be like when they return? Will they have transformed and combined into the super-powerful Ultra Dragon, as the legends say?

Dragons remain mysterious, but I believe my Father created those beautiful creatures for a reason. I do not know how or when they first came to the Ninjago Realm. I do not even know if the Spirit Coves actually exist, since no human has proven they have seen them.

A Master of Spinjitzu can be a dragon master. Can a man and a beast be perfect guardians of the world of Ninjago?

Years ago, I tasked four dragons, each related to one of the elements of creation, to guard the location of the Golden Weapons. When my students retrieved the weapons and their individual connections to the elements were revealed, the dragons and my students became linked. The dragons became an important form of transportation for the ninja, as well as powerful allies.

Dragons can travel to the Underworld. Is it possible for them to travel through other realms?

But there are also Elemental Dragons, pure beings of elemental energy that can be summoned after an Elemental Master has unlocked their True Potential. Much later, when the master has faced their greatest fear, they can summon their elemental dragon - which is a manifestation of their courage and ability to triumph over doubt.

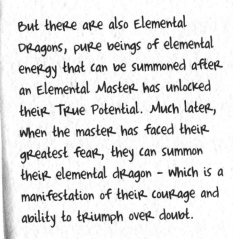

The energy of dragons cannot be curbed, but it is possible to control it through a special bond established between a human and a beast. It's not necessary to be spiritually mature to do that. I'm proud of my students, the Spinjitzu ninja in training, who managed to forge that bond.

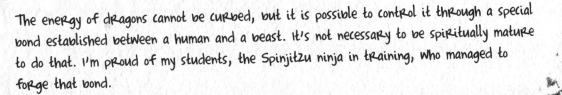

THE UNLIKELIEST NINJA

"IT IS NOT THE SIZE OF THE NINJA IN THE FIGHT, IT'S THE SIZE OF THE FIGHT IN THE NINJA."

The newest, youngest and smallest of my students certainly was the least expected. He is my nephew, Lloyd Garmadon.

I have met Lloyd - my brother Garmadon and Misako's son. The boy had really wanted to be a villain to make his father proud. Still, I felt there was good in him, which he sometimes cannot hide. I'm sure he gets that from his mother. Sometimes I think of him as of the son I could have had.

Lloyd went on to free the long-imprisoned Serpentine tribes, hoping he could command them, but they turned on him.

He then decided to be good rather than evil, and had just begun his Spinjitzu training with us, when he was recaptured by the Serpentine and forced to serve them. I feel Lloyd will be a very important member of my ninja team. I must rescue him, but I will need help from my brother ...

What a surprise!

PROGRESS REPORT

"THERE COMES A TIME WHEN WE ALL MUST GROW."

My heart bursts with pride! During their quest to recover the Four Fang Blades, my students overcame personal obstacles and reached their True Potential, finding their elemental powers within Spinjitzu. I wish my Father could have seen this!

Zane learned of his true history and accepted it. He can control ice and create amazing objects out of it!

He is also making the Destiny's Bounty very cold!

Jay stopped pretending and realised that he just needed to be himself. Now the Elemental Master of Lightning can project powerful bolts of electricity!

Jay still doubts himself from time to time ... but Nya always helps him to regain confidence.

Cole made peace with his father, who had wanted him to be a performer. Then, he claimed his destined mantle as Elemental Master of Earth, able to control rocks and soil.

Kai remained impatient but managed to unlock his True Potential when he understood the value of teamwork, and that his team's destiny is to protect Lloyd ... the future Green Ninja. Now he controls the power of his element – fire.

Nya has yet to unlock her potential and she still needs training – but she's working hard ...

FORMING THE GREEN NINJA

"NINJA SHARPENS NINJA!"

When I finally discovered that the prophesied Green Ninja was my nephew Lloyd, I was overjoyed. Then I realised that the final battle between the Dark Lord and the Green Ninja will, in fact, be a battle fought by father and son! My heart is broken. Will the boy stand up to the challenge? Will I be able to prepare him?

Lloyd must train with the team and unlock his True Potential. My skills as a teacher have never been more needed. My ninja and I will do our best to make the Green Ninja ready to face his destiny!

LLOYD'S DAILY
TRAINING SCHEDULE

5:00 am: Wake up

5:15 am: Breakfast

6:00 am: Stretching, rotation and balance exercises – supervised by Kai

8:00 am: Endurance hike at top speed – with Zane

11:00 am: Free running and ballet class (to develop agility) – with Cole

12:00 pm: Lunch – with the team

1:00 pm: Scroll and book study – alone or with my brother

3:15 pm: Rooster chasing (to develop speed) plus more rotation exercises

6:00 pm: Sparring (assign an off-duty ninja to be a sparring partner)

6:30 pm: Dinner – with the team

7:45 pm: Obstacle course (including more rotation and balance exercises) – supervised by Kai

9:00 pm: Recreation – with Jay

9:30 pm: Bed (assign Zane to do the bedtime story reading)

The Green Ninja should be totally committed to his Spinjitzu training, but he shouldn't train beyond his strength. You can derive satisfaction from broadening your possibilities.

Can I get him ready in time? Are we pushing him too hard?

When the time comes to fight the Darkness, I do hope Lloyd is properly trained in Spinjitzu – for our enemy is strong. Yet, my heart aches at the thought that the evil we will be fighting is my brother, too. Destiny plays cruel tricks on us ...

NEARLY HUMAN

"YOU CAN BE MADE OF METAL AND STILL HAVE A GREAT HEART."

4

Zane is the embodiment of what can be achieved through practising Spinjitzu. During our recent struggle to keep the Fang Blades from the Serpentine, he has discovered he is a Nindroid. It was not easy for him to accept the truth about himself, but eventually he understood that everyone is unique and has their own undiscovered potential.

I had observed Zane long before I approached him. I knew he was one of a kind, just like the other ninja I wanted to recruit. The day we met, before I asked him to join the team, he was sitting at the bottom of a lake, testing his resistance. I realised he was ready to start his Spinjitzu training.

It does explain why he was so special!

After overcoming his initial shock, Zane noticed a memory switch in some blueprints of himself, and located it in his chest. When he reactivated it, his memories returned. Zane had been built by Dr Julien, who had treated him like a son. Before Dr Julien passed away, he turned off Zane's memory circuits to spare him the heartbreak he would feel.

But with his memories restored, Zane experienced that heartbreak, and felt stronger for having done so. Zane is grateful to be a unique Nindroid that can feel and experience friendship. We have all been unspeakably grateful to have Zane as a friend!

Before one can master Spinjitzu, one must completely accept one's self. I am proud of Zane for unlocking his True Potential.

DANGER, DANGER EVERYWHERE

"LISTEN TO YOUR HEART BUT BE GUIDED BY REASON."

Over the years, my study of Spinjitzu has taught me never to underestimate anyone as a potential enemy. Here are some great examples of this.

The evil Nindroids, constructed by tech genius Cyrus Borg to serve the Overlord, can appear mindless and not much of a threat. However, they are tougher and more agile than humans.
Yet, Nindroids are unable to gain strength from friendship and they're incapable of making sacrifices, which is where some of the Spinjitzu Masters' strengths lie.

Even the Mindroid proved surprisingly tough ... especially when teased about his size!

A Skulkin named Krazi is also an example of a surprising enemy. With his jester's hat and crazed demeanour, he might not seem dangerous, but Spinjitzu teaches us that unpredictable enemies are the most difficult to fight, and Krazi is certainly unpredictable.

Spinjitzu's strength also comes from the mind — and reason always defeats madness! It's great for overcoming an unpredictable enemy like this one!

Knowing your enemies' strengths and weaknesses, regardless of their size, is the key to finding a way to defeat them!

Monkey Wretch, the chief mechanic for Nadakhan's pirate crew, doesn't look menacing, but a Spinjitzu Master should never judge by appearances. Monkey Wretch's strength is not a warrior's strength, but as a brilliant engineer he has built many dangerous machines.

INNER STRENGTH

"FEAR CAN HOLD YOU BACK OR PUSH YOU FORWARD."

Spinjitzu shows us that, more than any Nindroid, Serpentine or Overlord, fear is a ninja's greatest enemy, because it holds us back from true greatness. I have taught my students that in order to become real masters they should start believing in themselves, face up to their fears and trust what their heart is saying.

COMMON FEARS:

1. Flying
2. Speaking in front of an audience
3. Heights
4. Clowns
5. The dark
6. Failing
7. Spiders
8. Flowers
9. Porridge for breakfast
10. Dogs
11. Dentists (especially the ones dressed as clowns)
12. Snakes

I spend much of the ninja's training time dealing with fear. Often, I will surprise them with what scares them most. Some are making great progress, but Jay still has a tendency to scream and run to his room. He will learn — these things take time.

If a ninja can face and understand their fears, they are less likely to interfere with them accomplishing their goal. Remembering to centre yourself when confronted with what scares you most is key. Nobody is free from fear. Even I fear I will fail others, my Father in particular. He may no longer be with me, but I still do not want to disappoint him or the expectations he had of me.

A NINJA'S APPEARANCE

"YOUR ENEMY MAY JUDGE YOU ON YOUR APPEARANCE, BUT YOU MUST ALSO SHOW THEM WHERE THE REAL STRENGTH LIES - INSIDE OF YOU."

To best practise Spinjitzu, a ninja's typical clothing, or gi, should be simple, functional and allow maximum movement. A hood lets the ninja see but does not reveal the ninja's identity. Boot soles are padded so the ninja may move silently. And the gi's three belts make sure a ninja's trousers don't fall down during a fight!

A Spinjitzu ninja is honourable!

In training, ninja wear special helmets, chest protectors and other padding so they do not accidentally sustain injury.

These outfits emphasize a ninja's abilities in battle: the tenacity of ice, the impetuosity of fire, the speed of lightning and the strength of the earth.

Rocks orbiting Cole when he is doing a Spinjitzu Tornado never seem to block his vision.

The ninja occasionally wear armoured suits for combat involving heavy weapons. These suits have reinforced shoulder plating, sheaths for weapons and masks that cover only the lower part of the face.

When fighting, Cole keeps his wallet under here.

When not in uniform, the ninja dress as typical young people so they don't call undue attention to themselves.

HIDING IN PLAIN SIGHT

"MAKE YOUR ENEMY SEE WHAT YOU WANT HIM TO SEE."

Ninja must not only be smart and good fighters, they must also be quick-thinking. Many missions call for speed, stealth and disguise. Camouflage is an art within the art of Spinjitzu.

I'm proud of my students who have practised Spinjitzu's art of disguise in many different ways. When Nadakhan's crew took over the *Misfortune's Keep*, the ninja boarded it disguised as pirates ...

My students have also improvised disguises, creatively using materials at hand. They once cobbled together Stone Warrior disguises to sneak into Lord Garmadon's camp when he was still on Dark Island.

Nya has proven quite skilled at all manner of disguises. She posed as a Kabuki performer to blend in with Master Chen's entourage to help her fellow ninja. She also designed and built the DB X, and equipped it with software that allowed it to change its appearance — so the ninja could travel without being noticed.

TO WARM THE SOUL

4

"EVERY CUP OF TEA IS LIKE A JOURNEY IN ONE'S MIND."

When our world is in peril, a true Master of Spinjitzu takes no rest and fights until the agents of darkness are pushed back. However, there are moments when one needs to stop, relax, regain strength and reflect upon the surrounding world through meditation.

My preferred method of relaxation is making and drinking tea.

Tea making is an art just like Spinjitzu. It requires concentration and patience. Not only is the temperature of the water important, but the timing and technique used to steep the leaves and extract the flavour is crucial. I was amazed to realise how much I had learnt about rotation when stirring my tea ...

Mystake's Tea Shop

The different kinds of tea, able to satisfy the most sublime tastes, are plentiful and some have magical qualities. There is the tea that can speed up the aging process or the tea that helps one forget certain events (highly desirable, but rarely available). When made properly, some teas allow you to transport yourself across enormous distances, and between realms (a comfortable method of travelling for a Spinjitzu Master, I must admit). These can all be bought in Mystake's Tea Shop.

I have often dreamed of opening my own tea shop. I look forward to making my own blends and showing customers the delights and benefits of tea.

I've been told about a type of tea that helps grow facial hair. Who would need such tea?

EVERYONE HAS POTENTIAL

"THE ONLY CONSTANT IS CHANGE."

Spinjitzu teaches us to recognise potential, even in our enemies. Someone who is our adversary today might become our friend tomorrow. Life has proven many times that everyone deserves a second chance.

Here are some examples:

When we met Lloyd, he was our enemy. Initially he allied with the Serpentine, but when he discovered their evil nature he joined me and even sacrificed his youth to become the Green Ninja.

Lloyd's father (and my brother) Garmadon, experienced several changes of heart. Initially, he was pure of spirit and a devoted student of Spinjitzu. But after being bitten by the Great Devourer, his spirit was poisoned and he became evil. Later, when his son was in peril, Garmadon returned to the side of good and gave his life to save the realm of Ninjago.

Another example is my first Spinjitzu student, named Morro. I suspected he might be the Green Ninja, but when we learned he was not, Morro couldn't believe it. He wanted to prove that I was wrong so he left the temple and became my fierce enemy. Nevertheless, later on it turned out he wasn't entirely evil, as he returned on the Day of the Departed to help me.

Nothing remains the same forever. Change is a part of everything. A student of Spinjitzu must be open to change and flexible enough to deal with it.

AIRJITZU

All new martial arts can be traced back to Spinjitzu. The one created by Master Yang is a perfect example. Yang was a keen student of Spinjitzu. Who trained him, I don't know. But, like me, he was also extremely interested in the possibilities and powers of Spinjitzu. He carefully studied it and developed his own movement called Airjitzu.

An ancient parchment containing the secrets of the martial arts discipline of Airjitzu. Written by Yang, the scroll resides in the Ancient Library of Domu.

Jay insists on calling Airjitzu "Cyclon-Do".

Users of Airjitzu create elemental tornadoes that allow them to fly for a short time.

Important: To maintain an Airjitzu Tornado, keep legs tucked in during flight.

Important: Be aware of weather conditions before forming tornadoes.

Although many of his deeds may not be glorious examples to follow, Master Yang will always be remembered and highly esteemed for developing Airjitzu. I am confident that there are also other martial art forms related to Spinjitzu. As a student of Spinjitzu, I must continue documenting my Father's work.

MUSCLE IN MIND

"YOU MUST TURN THEIR GREATEST STRENGTH INTO THEIR GREATEST WEAKNESS."

Spinjitzu teaches us that what may seem to be a weakness can be turned into a strength. Cole's story, after he had become a ghost, shows that.

Cole: Normal

Cole: Ghost

Cole found himself trapped inside Yang's Haunted Temple, the old Temple of Airjitzu, at sunrise and as the legends foretold, he was transformed into a ghost. He became depressed, believing that as a ghost, he could no longer be a part of the ninja team.

Nya suggested that rather than dwell on what he could not do, Cole should find other ways to help. Cole learned that he could possess materials and objects, as well as pass through walls. These proved crucial in defeating both Morro and Nadakhan.

Even a small impediment can be used to one's advantage. Once I got the hiccups during a fight and I used it to deceive my opponent. I faked an extra hiccup, during which I delivered an unexpected blow!

While returning to his human form, Cole unlocked a new elemental power – the Earth Punch – that he is now struggling to harness.

Fumbling speech in a time of crisis can also add to the time it takes to convey information ... and help gain precious time before reinforcements arrive.

Never forget: A weakness only becomes a weakness if you let it.

DIFFERENT WARRIORS, DIFFERENT WAYS

"MANY ROADS MAY LEAD TO THE SAME DESTINATION."

Simple and light

The samurai and the ninja are very different. The former rely on their extraordinary weapon skills; the latter derive strength from their bodies and minds.

Great warriors never miss an opportunity to learn and develop their skills. The samurai and the ninja can learn from each other. Spinjitzu encourages an incessant search for inspiration.

Flexible and stylish

Quiet and easily stored

Helmet – elaborate but makes vision difficult

Armour – protective but restricts movement

Samurai sword – dangerous but requires time and space to use

Although the heavy armour never affected Nya's performance, I'm happy she has passed on her Samurai X legacy to someone else ...

For a long time, Nya fought alongside the ninja as the mysterious Samurai X. She managed that role very well because she is an inventive engineer and loves upgrading weapons. It is difficult for her to follow the path of the Master of Water without the mechanised armour she had as Samurai X, but I am certain she will find her inner strength and confidence to become an excellent Spinjitzu ninja.

ONE ART, MANY MASTERS

"SPINJITZU REFLECTS OUR QUALITIES AND PASSIONS. OUR DIFFERENCES ARE SHOWN IN HOW WE MASTER SPINJITZU."

- My Father was full of secrets. He never told me whom he had trained before me and Garmadon. Over the years, I have trained a select few, but somehow others across Ninjago Island have learned Spinjitzu as well.

Note for the future: Assemble a list of all known Spinjitzu Masters. Who are allies and who are enemies?

My brother, Garmadon, was a great Spinjitzu Master. Could he have taught the dark variant of Spinjitzu to others before he was banished to the Underworld? I trained Misako before she married Garmadon and we grew close during that time.

Nadakhan was a powerful, evil djinn with the ability to grant wishes. His henchman, Doubloon, once studied Spinjitzu, but that was long before he became a thief. Caught stealing from the *Misfortune's Keep*, Nadakhan made him into a mute, two-faced pirate.

Never, EVER, steal from a djinn.

Once Doubloon became Nadakhan's thug, he used Spinjitzu Tornadoes in combat. That made me incredibly sad. Spinjitzu is not for pirates and thieves.

LEARNING FROM MISTAKES

"DO NOT WISH, ACT – ONLY THIS WAY CAN YOU INFLUENCE THE PRESENT."

It is important to have ambition and to dream, but wishful thinking can lead to disaster. Our recent clash with a wish-granting djinn proved that I have not spent enough time teaching my students the dangers of wishful thinking. This mistake turned out to be a hard lesson for me and the ninja ...

Nya and Delara looked almost exactly alike.

When Nadakhan, the powerful, evil djinn I have spoken of, escaped captivity from the Teapot of Tyrahn and kidnapped Nya, he intended to marry her and return the soul of his lost love, Delara, to Nya's body. If he'd succeeded, it would have given Nadakhan unlimited wishes of his own and made him invincible.

Nadakhan was not a foe that could be easily defeated with kicks and punches. He would cunningly trick his opponents into granting them wishes that turned against them. But my ninja and I failed to find the cleverest way to prevail within Spinjitzu and we fell into the djinn's trap when we recklessly wished for things or abilities we couldn't have. Fortunately, thanks to Jay's last selfless wish, Nadakhan's threat was obviated.

Were it not for Jay, we would have been trapped in the Djinn Blade forever.

The clash with the wish-granting djinn was a lesson learned the hard way. The art of Spinjitzu focuses on harnessing the present. Of course, dreaming is important, but wishful thinking gives you nothing in return. Therefore, we all should reflect upon these simple truths:

1. Being a Master of Spinjitzu is not about words but actions.
2. Make your dreams come true through your actions.
3. Think twice before you act, or you could get into trouble.

STRONGER TOGETHER

"SEARCH FOR THE POWER WITHIN, THEN REALISE THE GREATNESS WITHIN EACH OTHER."

I wrote earlier of not underestimating your enemies. The same can be said for your friends. Spinjitzu makes it very clear that everyone has a skill. Your friends can help you reach your goals.

This Spinjitzu teaching was evident during the battle with Nadakhan. Jay felt that because he was the only ninja with a wish left, it was up to him, alone, to save the world of Ninjago. However, he had other allies who were more than willing to help him.

The one-legged Captain Soto was experienced in fighting pirates; Skylor had the unique ability to absorb the power of others; Echo Zane was a rusty machine programmed like Zane to protect those who cannot protect themselves; Ronin was a thief but he was resourceful and crafty ...

Never forget one of the most valuable Spinjitzu teachings: No ninja stands alone.

... and the grumpy old Ninjago City Police Commissioner was determined and committed to do the right thing.

Knowing their obvious flaws and weaknesses, Jay was also able to see the great potential in each of them. By standing together, they made a formidable team that helped Jay free the ninja from the Djinn Blade.

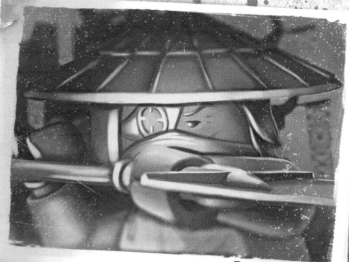

Ronin

ALL AROUND THE WORLD

"SPINJITZU IS EVERYWHERE."

Ninjago Island, the home of Spinjitzu, is a remarkable place full of many wonders. It is a vast land, with mountains and seas, forests, deserts, villages, cities, temples and caves. Many are important in its history and lore. I have travelled far and wide and discovered how beautiful my Father's creation really is. Some places are worth highlighting.

DARK ISLAND

The world of Ninjago originally consisted of one huge island. When the Overlord's Stone Army threatened to overwhelm the world with darkness, my Father split the island in half and Dark Island became the Overlord's territory. The island sank to the seabed and remained underwater for years, only to resurface when Lord Garmadon arrived.

THE HOLY CITY OF DOMU

This ancient library holds many books and documents of great importance to the world of Ninjago, such as Master Yang's Scroll of Airjitzu.

Note to self: Must return overdue books.

On quiet days, I have been known to sneak off to the city's Mega Monster Amusement Park to ride the Spinning Teacups.

NINJAGO CITY

Ninjago City is Ninjago Island's largest metropolis, with everything a big city has to offer. Be sure to visit Mystake's excellent tea shop and see the magnificent Titanium Statue in the park.

JAMANAKAI VILLAGE

This peaceful village near the Mountains of Impossible Height was a key location of conflict during the Serpentine Wars. When it's not under attack, it is a popular holiday spot.

GLACIER BARRENS

This frozen mountain range is where you can find the Tomb of the Hypnobrai tribe, but that doesn't keep the annual Ninjaball Run Race from running through its peaks.

REMEMBERING OUR FATHERS

"IF WE NEVER LOOK TO THE PAST, WE CANNOT ENVISION THE FUTURE."

The Day of the Departed always makes me reflect on the past and the people close to my heart who are no more. Every time I think about my father, I realise I would give anything to be able to see and talk to him again. And when I look at my nephew, Lloyd, I understand he must feel the same about his father ...

I have not missed the evil spirits from Ninjago Island's history that were summoned this year by the ghost of Master Yang to fight us. Today, my ninja and I are particularly grateful for the knowledge and skills we have acquired, thanks to my father.

Kai and Nya faced Master Chen. Following Spinjitzu teachings on how to take advantage of the enemy's weakness, they defeated Chen whose weakness was overconfidence.

CRyptor fought Zane in Birchwood Forest. The ninja tricked the evil spirit into destroying the mannequin he had possessed with his own Techno-Blade and, without a body to house him, CRyptor's spirit fled.

Many a time have I told my students that the power of Spinjitzu also comes from friendship. Obviously, Jay has learned his lesson well by teaming up with Ronin to fight Samukai and his skeletons at Ed and Edna's junkyard.

Kozu and a squad of Stone Warriors attacked the ninja's friend Dareth, but he remembered the Helmet of Shadows and used its powers to take command of the warriors, forcing them to destroy Kozu's mannequin ... and their own.

Dareth fancies himself the 'Brown Ninja'. But he is no ninja, and he will never be one, unless someone teaches him. It will not be me!

Pythor teamed with the spirits and nearly crushed Lloyd under the severed head of a giant statue, but with Misako's encouragement to believe in his powers, Lloyd rallied the power of the Green Ninja to turn the tables.

I was faced with the spirit of Morro, but rather than fight me, he helped us defeat the ghosts. Perhaps it was his way of making up for letting down his old teacher, years ago.

This year's Day of the Departed has been special. I saw my students putting my Spinjitzu teachings into practice. Once again, I realised how important my Father's legacy is. I wish he were here to see that the work of his life has been carried on. I wish my brother was here, too ...

But I do not despair, because I remember my history. Garmadon has returned to me before when I thought him gone forever. Perhaps he will do so again ... And I still have Lloyd – I can see so much of his father and grandfather in him!

AN ALLIANCE OF ELEMENTS

"A STRAW ALONE IS WEAK, BUT MANY WOVEN TOGETHER CAN BE AS STRONG AS STEEL."

"Ninja sharpens ninja," my Father always said. And that old man was right. Now I am an old man myself. But the curious thing is that no matter how old we get, we keep forgetting and learning this again. A Spinjitzu ninja needs strong friendships and alliances, people you can trust, because one day, you will need to stand united to fight a common threat.

The original Elemental Masters were the First Spinjitzu Master's guardians. Most of these men and women were not Spinjitzu ninja, but rather skilled fighters whom my Father granted special elemental powers to. The Elemental Alliance was born.

Generations later, my brother and I fought side by side with the Elemental Masters in the Serpentine Wars. After that, there was a time of peace. When the Hands of Time, Krux and Acronix, rebelled against us, the Elemental Alliance reunited to save the Realm of Ninjago.

My friends, Ray and Maya (Kai and Nya's parents), used Chrono-Steel to forge special weapons — Time Blades that could absorb one's elemental power. Only with those unique weapons were Garmadon and I able to defeat the evil Time Twins.

There are four Time Blades:

- Forward Blade
- Reversal Blade
- Slow-Mo Blade
  - Pause Blade

When all four are put together, the Time Blades hold the power to time travel!

POWER CORRUPTS

"TIME IS THE THREAD THAT SEWS
THE FABRIC OF THE UNIVERSE TOGETHER."

Time can change villains into heroes and heroes into villains. Our recent confrontation with Krux and Acronix, the Hands of Time, proves this.

Spinjitzu warns that power can corrupt anyone, even the most warm-hearted people. Krux and Acronix had the strongest powers of all members of the Elemental Alliance. Over time, they started to believe that their immense power entitled them to rule the realm of Ninjago.

End of the
Serpentine Wars

Krux and Acronix
betray the
Elemental Alliance

War breaks out

Luckily, Garmadon and I foiled the brothers' plans. Knowing how dangerous the Time Blades could be and that time was too great a power for anyone to control, we threw the weapons into a Temporal Vortex. We hoped they would be lost forever, but the Hands of Time leapt in after them and disappeared.

Acronix has arrived from the past. For him, it was a quick journey into a distant future. Now, facing me, an old man, he wanted to finish what we had started. But this encounter did not go as well as I might have hoped ...

Spinjitzu teaches us that time is a river that flows only forward, but the Time Twins can speed ahead of the current, or travel back to a place already visited. Time travel is too dangerous. You change anything, you change everything ...

Ray and Maya forge the four
Time Blades from Chrono-Steel

Time Blades thrown
into Time Vortex

Krux and Acronix leap into Time
Vortex to reclaim Time Blades

We use the Time Blades to
absorb Hands of Time's powers

Note to self: Talk to Lloyd, it's
very important that he ...

FOCUS

"SHARPEN YOUR MIND AS WELL AS YOUR SPINJITZU."

The path to becoming a Spinjitzu Master is long and winding. The greatest challenge is to start controlling oneself, so a ninja must learn the art of concentration and move towards attaining inner balance.

Over time, I have come to recognise my students' greatest distractions. However, the aim is not to make them abandon these distractions, but rather to teach them to recognise situations in which the distractions shatter their inner peace.

Kai's primary distraction is anger. When he becomes upset, he loses his ability to help the team. He must stay focused on the team's goals.

...ne is a Nindroid ...d humans may not ...ways understand ...s behaviour. He ...cuses a lot on his ...nse of humour, so ...joke can make him ...e concentration.

Mistakes distract Cole. If he fails, the events play over and over in his mind, and he doesn't pay attention to what he's doing. Unless a ninja has a Time Blade, the past cannot be changed — the present is what matters most.

...y is often distracted ... Nya, comics and ...iny things. Giving ...m duties crucial to ...ssions keeps him on ...ack.

Lloyd's major distraction was his relationship with his father. He and Garmadon made peace before Garmadon sacrificed himself to save the world of Ninjago.

...ya is often distracted ... Jay. To keep her ...cused, I remind ...r of her ...rents' focus ... protecting my ...p to the Golden ...eapons.

As my journey towards the mastery of Spinjitzu continues, I strive to eliminate all distraction from my life. Well ... a good pot of tea can still turn my head on occasion.

AMONG THE PURE-HEARTED SPINJITZU ENDURES

"A WATCHFUL EYE NEVER SLEEPS."

If I have learned one thing in my lifelong study of Spinjitzu, it is that a ninja never comes to a point where he can say he has learned all that there is to know. A true master should always continue their quest, even when they are nearing the end of their days.

The Book of Spinjitzu is my legacy, which I will eventually pass to my successors and which they will one day pass to theirs — because the world of Ninjago will always need protectors. My Father's teachings and now mine, must always live on.

If you are reading these words it means that I am not here any more – or that somehow this book has been lost.

Life is a great adventure. I have devoted mine to studying the secrets of Spinjitzu and I discovered that they can be of value not only to ninja, but to all. The essence of Spinjitzu lies in the ability to get to know and accept oneself, because self-worth and inner balance are what helps each of us weather adversities and gain confidence.

BE NINJA.

May your path be a long, healthy and happy one. If my teachings and reflections come in handy on your life's journey, please do remember me sometimes – perhaps over a nice cup of tea …